la carreta made a U-turn

Tato Laviera

Arte Público Press
Houston
Texas
1992

upport for the press of the Lila
Andrew Mellon Foundation and
eral agency.

Arte Público Press
University of Houston
Houston, Texas 77204-2090

Cover design by Mark Piñón.
Front cover photo by Dominique.

Laviera, Tato.
    La carreta made a U-turn / Tato Laviera. – 2nd ed.
        p.   cm.
    English and Spanish.
    ISBN 1-55885-064-3
    1. Puerto Ricans—New York (N.Y.)—Poetry. 2. New York (N.Y.)—Poetry.
I. Title.
PS3562.A849C3 1992
811'.54–dc20   92-38421

                                                                    CIP

CONTENTS

Metropolis Dreams

Loisaida Streets: Latinas Sing

El Arrabal: Nuevo Rumbón

Foreword to the 1992 Edition

La Carreta Made a U-Turn was the first book published by Arte Público Press. Its impact was so great that almost immediately upon publication it was the subject of a forty-page article in the respected journal *Daedalus*. Over the years, it has also been the subject of numerous reviews and literary studies, and Tato Laviera has become almost synonymous with Nuyorican/Hispanic and bilingual literature. Laviera has produced three other successful books of poems, all published by Arte Público Press. Since 1979, *La Carreta Made a U-Turn* has gone through five reprint editions; the present is the sixth and first completely new edition. Without a doubt, Tato Laviera's *La Carreta Made a U-Turn* is the most popular and most widely read book of poetry by a U.S. Hispanic author.

It was not only the popularity of *La Carreta Made a U-Turn* among critics and public that firmly planted the identity of Tato Laviera and Arte Público Press on the literary landscape. It was the book's clear enunciation of a U.S. Hispanic esthetic, its unashamed proclamation of a bilingual-bicultural, working-class, Afro-European-Amerindian-New World literature. The roots of all that Arte Público Press has been able to produce since 1979 are to be found in this marvelous, visionary—but modest—collection of incredibly original poems by one of the most gifted synthesizers of the oral and written traditions of literature.

Arte Público Press, then as now, was humbled that so talented an artist and such an important book would be entrusted to its care. That it was the first book in our history was either fate or blind luck. That Arte Público Press would have as its first and greatest ambassador such a dynamic and beloved figure as Tato Laviera was again incredibly fortunate.

With this 1992 edition, Tato, we wish you many more years of reprints and editions. May Arte Público Press always fulfill your vision for it and for our literature as a whole, just as all of your poetry has inspired the press to continue to promote our literary and cultural identity. Thank you.

Nicolás Kanellos
Publisher

Foreword

The 1953 production of René Marqués' play, *La Carreta*, inaugurated a new era in Puerto Rican letters in which the language and experience of the Puerto Rican working class were validated as literary and artistic matter. The play recreated in symbolic and dramatic terms the Puerto Rican diaspora and fixed in the collective subconscious of Puerto Ricans indelible images of dislocation from the countryside, slum life in San Juan and migration to New York. Even moreso it succeeded in capturing the essence of the migratory experience of a colonized people through characters and situations that today are immediately recognizable to peoples throughout the world who are caught between the frontiers of culture and politics.

Marqués' vision of Puerto Ricans in New York was soon copied and embellished many times over, its truths often becoming sociologic commonplaces and media stereotypes that at times fed islanders' already tarnished image of their "acculturated" countrymen who were living stateside. Laviera's *La Carreta Made a U-turn* here forms a fourth act to the play. The protagonists are the Puerto Ricans who did not or could not return to the island to cultivate the land, resist cultural intrusion from without, and dream of shedding the bonds of colonialism.

More than twenty years later, Laviera, through the poetics of bilingualism, is helping to reshape the consciousness created by *La Carreta* in affirming the existence of a culturally and psychologically whole people that is strong enough to bring together two languages, two experiences, two worlds. To be Nuyorican is to be universal, is to be existentially wired to men of different colors and tongues the world over: Spanish-speakers, English-speakers, and peoples anywhere whose existence cannot be categorized or labeled by language, nationality or race. To the mestizo, the mulatto, and half breed. More than that, to all Americans that, whether they realize it or not, are living in a mestizo/mulatto civilization that enjoys the cultural heritage of Africa, the Americas, Asia and Europe. To the great salseros and jazz musicians who, long before the poets, conjugated the sounds of three continents into the heartbeat of a people. To all peoples who have been uprooted from their land and have had to witness their own children's severed roots. To all peoples struggling to create themselves. To the strong women who personify their creative spirit. Finally, to the town poets, barroom singers, and front porch philosophers whose oral tradition has kept the culture ringing in the air to be captured once again and recreated on paper by modern troubadours like Tato Laviera.

Nicolás Kanellos, Publisher
Arte Público Press, 1979

la carreta made a U-turn

Metropolis Dreams

para ti, mundo bravo

in the final analysis
i am nothing but a historian
who took your actions
and jotted them on paper

therefore making you
the source, the strength,
the base of my inspirations

in the final analysis
i know that the person
in this society most
likely to suffer ...

> is you, out there
> sometimes living the
> life of a wandering nomad
> to taste the breadcrumbs
> of survival ...

one thing though,
if we ever meet
and you overpower me,
i would mention a book
by dostoevsky which
you have not read

and don't think because i passed
the evening junior high school
exam that i am more educated
than you

i still have plenty of room
to grow, check me out
and straighten me ...
don't cliché me ...
i might get angry now

but in the final analysis
i'll appreciate it, thank you.

even then he knew

papote sat on the stoop
a social club   plays   che che colé
a pentecostal church sings   hallelujah
the sunday garbage   three days old
          a burned car
yards full of junk   an addiction center
drunks on every   empty   milk box
velloneras   parties   screams
          firecrackers
air   infected   with   summer heat
junkies of   all kinds   all ages
papote sat on the stoop
puerto rican flags   for patches in the asses
political   prisoners   posters   destroyed
no stars   no skies   no room to breathe
papote sat on the stoop
miseducated   misinformed
a blown-up   belly   of   malnutrition
papote sat on the stoop
of an abandoned building
he decided to go nowhere

frío

35 mph winds
& the 10 degree
weather
penetrated the pores
of our windows
mr. steam rested for
the night
the night we most
needed him

everybody arropándose
on their skin blankets
curled-up like the embryo
in my mother's womb
a second death birth
called nothingness

& the frío made more
asustos in our empty
stomachs
        the toilet has not
        been flushed for
        three days

a tight touch

inside the crevice
deeply hidden in basement land
inside an abandoned building
the scratching rhythm of dice
percussion like two little bongos
in a fast mambo.

quivering inside this tiny ray
of sun struggling to sneak in.

the echo of the scent attracted
a new freedom which said, "we are
beautiful anywhere, you dig?"

my graduation speech

i think in spanish
i write in english

i want to go back to puerto rico,
but i wonder if my kink could live
in ponce, mayagüez and carolina

tengo las venas aculturadas
escribo en spanglish
abraham in español
abraham in english
tato in spanish
"taro" in english
tonto in both languages

how are you?
¿cómo estás?
i don't know if i'm coming
or si me fui ya

si me dicen barranquitas, yo reply,
"¿con qué se come eso?"
si me dicen caviar, i digo,
"a new pair of converse sneakers."

ahí supe que estoy jodío
ahí supe que estamos jodíos

english or spanish
spanish or english
spanenglish
now, dig this:

hablo lo inglés matao
hablo lo español matao
no sé leer ninguno bien

so it is, spanglish to matao
what i digo
         ¡ay, virgen, yo no sé hablar!

angelito's eulogy in anger

angelito is my brother
can you undestand?
angelito is my brother

not that bro talk we misuse
but the real down
brother-blood-salsa   sangre de madre

angelito is my brother
dancing slow curves of misery
nodding slow-motion tunes
of alcohol dynamic soul   arrastrándose por las calles
                                     con su andar de angel-loco

standing on the usual
corner the talk of all
the affliction in the ghetto:
                                     se llevó el radio
                                     me escondió los cheques
                                     me quitó la cartera
                                     se robó el tique del ponchop

                                     pero angelito lo pusieron
                                     ahí mami, me entiendes

angelito was being sponsored
by soft legislators and by
the multi-million dollars
the racket is worth annually
and all of you loved the godfather
the all-time ghetto best film forever

                                     me entiendes, papi
                                     angelito lo tenían ahí
                                     amedrentándoles las venas
                                     mocosas sucias que
                                     le imprentaron
                                     a ese hermano mío
                                     de sange vinagrosa
                                     húmeda de esa sangre

descalza aguada
que cambió de roja a blanca

angelito was angered
by the teacher
the preacher
the liberal
the social worker
the basketball coach
that mistreated him and
didn't let him express
his inner feelings

a angelito le hicieron un trabajo
espiritual le echaron agua
maldita le mezclaron sus buenos
pensamientos le partieron el
melodioso cantar del cucurucú
en su cantar en brujos

angelito didn't get the chance
to receive an education or to
graduate from basic english
courses   no lo querían curar
because of that once a junkie
always a junkie theory i was
taught ten years ago when
heroine had not yet invaded the
wired fences of queens. all of
a sudden drugs reach queens blvd.
and all kinds of addiction cen-
ters popped off on my block to
cure them

y tú, condenao madre y padre
a veces te digo,
por dejarte convencer
sus cabezas
por sus caprichos
de más dinero
por parar de sembrar guineos
por traernos a este

maldito sitio
donde nos ultrajaron
los bichos de varones
las tetas llenas de leche
de mi abuela
los poderosos pezones
de aquella jibarita
que se meneaba poderosamente
que me hubiese
gustado agarrarla
con mucho gusto . . . .
ahora, a esa jibarita,
me la tienen
como tecata flaca
perdida en su desaliento
andando de prostituta
abriéndole las patas
al viejo palo de mapo

and the other junkies
the real junkies of the
true definition of the
word junkie (the ones
who stumped your community
with high class hopes shaded
by lack of real attention)
they profited died fat cats
and bought their way into
heaven

nunca los oí decir ni hablar
nada sobre ellos
zánganos aguajeros
sigan tomando cervezas
sigan mirando novelas
sigan criticándose uno a otro
sigan echándole la culpa sólo
a los padres

angelito sabía todo esto
entonces él en la perdición
de su muerte está más despierto

que ustedes. angelito me dijo
todo esto. cuando yo hablo
contigo
lo único que
oigo es el score de los mets

and the rest of you
so-called pretty looking
bad so bad dumb young
spics are sleeping underneath
the $45 price of your pants

a speech outside the jail

i'm caught in dead lock
between freedom and fear

tight as the rust
that's buried in-
side the bolted
screws of the
holland tunnel

& the erosion
of polluted waters
will dissolve me
in slow-motion
agony, as in
the process of
wrinkled veins
mellowing into
softness

i'm caught in dead lock
between freedom and fear:
inevitable companions
in the process of
thought, for freedom
as the unrestricted
improvisation feeds
the fear which is
the vanguard restriction
that molds & modifies
the original thought

perhaps those stained
by society because
of an unlawful action
upon readjusting, lose
the initial wisdom of
freedom & begin their
perceptions from fear

excommunication gossip

if it is dreams you seek
after your body is cremated
inside the grave of roofless
cemeteries.

if it is everlasting life
heaven or infinite salvation
you seek, don't cry in heaven
when you find out the lord
discriminated against minorities
if it is racism in earth you
encountered, there's a special place
for you in heaven, the official
laundromatician for virgin mary's
silk kotexes.

benditoizing the ingenious lord
who kept you secure thinking
about the sacred blessings
bestowed on them by a host

me caso en la hostia
me caso en la hostia
divina esa que trajo
muchos edificios fríos
pero el padre vivía en
la rectoría, y había mucha
agua caliente, y había mucha
agua caliente.

and the bishops
and the archbishops
and the cardinals
and the pope
slept in golden beds
i provided the good income

yes, i live on welfare
but those so-called princes
live on welfare of the people

praying contrition after contrition
and papi and myself never had anything
to say to each other ....
(yo se lo había dicho todo al condenao
padre ese de la iglesia)

now i look at my disassociation with
papi and i blame it on you sacerdote
(todo el cariño era para mami y papi
se jodía por mí, yo nunca le presté atención)

porque tenía muchos padrastros
mentales que me alejaban de mi papá
para que yo no conociera
el porqué de sus cortejas
el porqué de sus borracheras
el porqué de los golpes malditos
porque él estaba rechazando
estas maldiciones
estas contradicciones inconcientemente

muchas basuras	kyrie eleison
muchos robos	kyrie eleison
mucho frío	kyrie eleison
sin educación	christe eleison
sin viviendas	christe eleison
sin patria	christe eleison
orando	kyrie eleison
con hambre	kyrie eleison
sin nada	kyrie eleison

and i liked the organ
cause it reminded me
of the solemn tecato notes
i would hear in the high
mass of my building ...   a kind of motionless move
                                 a kind of seeing with eyes
                                 closed
                                 a kind of 78-speed record
                                 playing on 33

and the epistle letters
of st. paul were fabulous
the only letters
we received were dispossess
notes from the bolitero to the landlord
and everybody in between

i read a letter discharging me from school
i read a letter announcing the arrival of pedro's
    coffin from nam
i read a letter dated by mr. angel ruiz
    commissioner of the holy bible payments
    claiming my mother's favorite passage
    from her rented holy bible
i read a letter in which installment payments
    were after our family
i read a letter to subpoena my younger
    brother to court because he stole one
    lousy egg from the next door neighbor
    who had stolen it in la marketa

OREMUS

    may the sentiments
    of the people rise
    and become espiritistas
    to take care of our religious
    necessities ....
    y echar brujos de fufú y
    espíritus malos a los que
    nos tratan como naborías
    y esclavos ....
    and sentence them to hang
    desnudos tres días en orchard
    beach, pa que yemayá le saque
    sus maldades

subway song

strange women come down subway stairs
walking under realism, walking inside
the concrete streets.

the subway fan spreads
everybody's breath around,
people reading newspapers
not respecting each other
a long welfare turnstile of faces
seeking half minute stardom on token ads
reminding them of what they should be
  the virginia slim liberated woman
  walking the winchester man.

how far? really how far?
leaving my innocence on cold stoops,
why is america confused?
why does she adapt foreign modes
to escape her present reality?
why am i left alone as if i were
a token outside a telephone booth?

slowly beginning to hate the make-up girl
a certain nausea ... diarrhea
faces not integrating, and me, the between
of silent streets in nocturne caves
digging deep in faithful sleep i sing:

  nobody goes to east harlem in the morning
  nobody goes to the south bronx in the morning
  east harlem receives the subway with a sad face
  nobody wants to see beauty in the morning
  and the building on an empty lot disappears
  in the darknes of the sunny day.

  my eyes are closed
  my eyes are opened to see the dark world
  inside the above of my eyelids.

    i found the happy spirits

protecting me
singing to me
goofing with me.

something i heard

on the streets of san juan
muñoz marín stands on top
of an empty milk box
and brings his land, liberty,
bread message to a people
robbed of their existence.
napoleón's father attentively
listened as muñoz said, "independence is just around the
corner."

napoleón's father took it
literally, he went around
the corner and found a donkey
tied up to a pole.

against muñoz pamphleteering

and i looked into the dawn
inside the bread of land and liberty
to find a hollow sepulchre of words
words that i admired from my mother's eyes
words that i also imbedded as my dreams.

now i awake to find that the underneath
of your beautiful poetry pamphleteering
against the mob of stars took me nowhere
muñoz, took me nowhere, muñoz, nowhere
where i see myself inside a triangle
of contradictions with no firm bridges
to make love to those stars.

inside my ghetto i learned to understand
your short range visions of where you led us,
across the oceans where i talk about myself
in foreign languages, across where i reach
to lament finding myself re-seasoning my
coffee beans.

your sense of
stars landed me in a
north temperate uprooted zone.

the last song of neruda

tell me where the vest pocket park
poverty of america is found and i shall
expose the universal suffering
every decent man strives to
eradicate:

inside i transform my shadow
into a puddle of water
in a crowded street

from there i shall rejoice
the pains of those who step on me

the beggar steps on me
carries a piece of my soul
to a deserted street
along the way the penetrable
hole in his shoe makes me feel
calloused flesh hardened by all
those suffering steps

he takes me to the bowery
the house of moth smell
the disinfectant warehouse
where coats are stored during
summer, but here, in here,
beggars store themselves every day
the accumulation of rare dirt
assembling to soil the concrete earth

inside this assembly i shall declare
that my poetry bleeded from prostatic
cancer, and in exposing society's cancer
i found the illumination of my thoughts,
pero aun, the fallen are the purest of all

let my soul rest here on the bowery
let me create with the rarest earth

my original puddle was drained by the sun
but in my life the sun of
military fires ashed my last thoughts.

fighting

ceased to be physical
when i realized my natural
potential for dealing with
institutions on their own
word and logic turf,

ceased to be physical
as I realized
that Alvin Ailey makes
me appreciate the
modern
dance form which i
applauded because i
understood

ceased to be physical when
the power of my uneducated
prose illicited respect at a job
interview at livingston college

ceased to be physical
when i decided to stop downgrading
myself as i fused my
energies to create, to strive,
        to extend myself onto
                the largest horizon

then fighting became a constant
manifestation of my mind and my
body announcing the claim that
all of us are creative cocos

Loisaida Streets: Latinas Sing

virginity

lamentable for your many falls

i only wish, in love,
your virginity was lost,
love ... lost ... beautiful!

lamentable for your many falls

the ideal is to lose it young, away
from home, keeping it a secret,
feeling the passion, the look,
especially if both were virgins

lamentable for your many falls

virginity ... thirteen ... too old.

a message to our unwed women

tears
   dri
      p   quietly   cutting your
                             face temporarily

eyes   SWOLLEN   NOSE a long voyage of sufrimiento

tears roll d
          o
          w
          n .... and you cry so deep   ly
                             so hurt

about to give birth and the lover refuses
                   and your father accuses
                   and your friends
                         con esa mirada

tears
   dri
      p   quietly   in the dark room
                             you sleep

tears are there
in the morning   that morning
                       when you walked down
                       the tenements up
                       the streets to la bodega

"adiós, ¿y cuándo
te casastes?"

                     and they gave you
                     the half mirada
                     and you bit the tears
                     from showing up

you walked knowing eyes were talking
                     eyes were following
                     eyes were criticizing

"look at . . . .
she was such a good girl"
as if your life had stopped
as if you dropped an atom bomb
as if you had to walk in shame
as if
as if
as if

tears suddenly stopped
in the most majestic manner
that pleased only yourself
you quietly said:

        "i am now a true woman
        my child will not be called
        illegitimate
        this act was done with love
        with passion
        my feelings cannot be planned
        i will not let their innocence
        affect me
        i will have him, coño,
        because i want him
        because i feel this breast
        of life consoling
        my hurt, sharing my grief,
        if anybody does
        not accept it
        que se vayan pal . . . me entienden
                pal . . . lo oyen
                pal . . . me escuchan."

the sun radiated
the streets became alive
"to give birth A LA RAZA
is the ultimate that i can
ever give."

a sensitive bolero in transformation
(for anne sexton)

se   no

se   no

          breast
          breast

se   sensual
no   se
suspiro

          breast
          hard
          duro
          mistreated
          maltratado
          manoseado

seno
seno no se . . . .   han abierto
          se están
          desarrollando
          buscando
          la fuerza
          dios mío
          la fuerza
          de crear
          de despojar   ¡leche!   ¡leche!

el jugo that juices   the softest flow
          inside the veins
          of my heart—my
          definition of
          browness

seno

          my secluded eyes
          the darkest shade
          of tan the sun
          gives me

seno encarcelado

        solamente el sol
        me ha tratado suavemente,
        constantemente ... sola-
        mente el sol me ha dado
        energía

seno suave

        breast caliente
        creates all the
        moods   all the
        feelings of my colors

seno   my third and fourth eyes

my longing is the   meñique
        anular
        del corazón
        índice
        pulgar
        fingers of a hand
        treat my breasts as sculptures
        choreographing the mental and
        spiritual ballet that would
        make his lips and then his
        body define me in my barest
        nudity to make the contact
        of harvesting flowless energy
        in space

seno   sensual
seno   orgánico

        why then
        do you treat them
        just as breasts?

the song of an oppressor

simplemente maría
simplemente maría
maría maría

> Doña Eusebia's knees were eliminated
> simple
> her head an army boot upside down
> mente
> her tongue was out from exhaustion
> maría

they took advantage
simple
english was foreign to you
mente
era el goofer del landlord de nuestras vidas
maría

> the tv tube
> simple
> whose jeringuillas
> mente
> made us addicted de la mente
> maría

how was it done?   simplemente maría

the exploiter rang the cash
simple
registered on a plane
mente
to new york or his cadillac in queens
maría

> in my anger i replied
> mami mami
> looking at dead novelas
> about natacha
> about renzo the gypsy
> feeling sorry about

the poor maid
feeling sorry about
the way she's treated
like a dog
like a slave
mami mami
stop saying
ay benditos and lamentos
why?
because in real life,
natacha is you eres tú eres tú eres tú

simplemente maría
simplemente maría
maría maría

i turned off the tv and said:
madre madre madre mía
always suffering at the knees
of your children. playing
on broadway off off broadway
every day, far from movies
theatres luxury hotels
under the direct supervision
of the landlords of our lives
who yell, "TRABAJO CHIPE
PISS WORK UN CHAVO POR
CADA VEINTE TRAJES."

madre madre madre mía
living like a whore
to buy legal aid
from storefront lawyers
who tell your son
to plead guilty

madre madre madre mía
those crystallized dreams about
america cars homes fortunes
were buried inside the needle
of the singer machine

🍂 🍂 🍂 🍂 🍂 🍂 🍂 🍂

s-i-m-p-l-e-m-e-n-t-e-m-a-r-í-a
s-i-m-p-l-e-m-e-n-t-e-m-a-r-í-a

> mami, you sit so calmly
> looking at your novelas
> looking at your children
> caring so much for them
> your love as silent as the lead
> writing on paper
>> as natural as the falling
>> autumn leaves
>> as eternal as the rising moon
>> the setting sun

> mami, tears of sacrifice sanctify
> your delicate face, valley of tears
> in your heart
> mami, i love you
> this spirit of love gives me rancor
> and hatred, and i react to the song
> simplemente maría. but my anger,
> my hate
> is based on love, ultimate love of you!

> mami, you are my epitomy
>> but i shall be your sword

simplemente maría
simplemente maría
maría   maría

titi teita and the taxi driver

mire, señor, mis familiares no han venido,
estoy perdida en el aeropuerto,
pero, yo sé la dirección, la calle
watel estrí

no se apure, señora, yo la llevaré
deme 50 pesos.

la tecata

sighs in front of garbage:
slimy mucous saliva engages
into vowels of overdosed movements
(the slow passivity of eyes closing)
begins output of expressive energy,
horns and flutes coming out into
the windows playing her out into
making her una madama scratching
hair in slow motion tecato scars
arranging herself to be hidden
inside the basement out of touch
with the horns improvising on her
without coming out to guide her.

the suffering of ruth santiago sánchez

oh, but my days are spent
in spiritual anger hearing
the crusty cries of ghetto
hearts living underground

despite that fact that yesterday
humanless landlords brought
about housing destruction and today
i'm trying to preserve
eighteenth century abandoned
structures wearing the weight of so many
immigrants.

the immigrants are still coming
but the buildings are
speculated to exclude people.

soledad

people talk about loneliness

is only sexual companionship
that's soon forgotten

people talk about solitude

beneath its seven layers
nobody can talk about solitude

and soledad

well, there is no english
translation

nightcap

a retrieve back into
personal. usually no
holes barred. compatibility.
he wants.   she needs.
he needs.   she wants.

the games of love turned
romantic pinches.
the moon does not walk,
she does not dare to give out
a bad wave.

palm tree in spanglish figurines

slowly, as in son montuno,
she erases frustrated tears
from face to hand ... she dances ...

natural coconut rhythms
swaying soul essences
and latino salsa all
intertwine within her

ocean eyes followed
her bolero-slow sensual movements
in cha-cha turned sharp curves,
a mysterious cult
inside the feelings of
ancestral bomba and plena

the maunabo indian emerged from her hips

piñones was her face setting

eyes looking for turtle eggs
mouth tasting cangrejos
in madrugada's solemnity

ocean eyes followed
interacting   within
screaming   above
searching   underneath
her latin dance
her escape from the
tear that collapsed
into daylight's hands
creating happiness

the congas mujer

a new woman was born!
her outstretched hands
carried the echoes
of madness to far away ears
oppression and love merged
pain and happiness fused
cuchifritos and books raped each other
america the beautiful woman
also was a prostitute in disguise
all prostitutes became mary magdalenes
the complete change
the ultimate despojo of oppression released
machismo and respect confronted each other
the sound has been ignited!
the motor running at great speed!
hand-powered attitudes driving powerfully!
driving onto the physical self!
destroying it, constructing ...
a new woman! a new woman ...
she shouted, and danced, and cried openly
without any hesitation
without any fear
making everyone deal with her
a new woman! a new woman!
beyond the criticism of the people
to the true self
the self that cried independence!
the self that analyzed calling major surgery!
the self that looked at man admiringly, not possessively
the self that is the self that is the self that is

El Arrabal: Nuevo Rumbón

the new rumbón

congas   congas   congas
congas   congas   congas

desperate hands need a fix from
the healthy skin of the congas
congas the biggest threat to heroin
congas make junkies hands healthier

las venas se curan ligero
con las congas conguito congas
congueros salsa de guarapo
melao azucarero

congas on summer months
take the place of the winter
fire that the wino congregation
seeks, the fire . . .

que calienta los tecatos muertos de
frío en el seno de un verano

congas gather around

con un rumboncito caliente . . .
y ahí vienen los morenos
a gozar con sus flautas y su soul jazz

congas   congas
tecata's milk gets warmed
broken veins leave misery
hypodermic needles melt
from the voodoo curse
of the conga madness

the congas clean the gasses
in the air, the congas burn out
everything not natural to our people

congas strong cuchifrito juice
giving air condition to faces
unmolested by the winds and the

hot jungles of loisaida streets
chévere, rumbones, me afectó
me afectó, me afectó, me afectó

chévere   rumbones   me afectó.

felipe luciano i miss you in africa

hey you black smooth stallion!
hey you black smooth stallion!
hey you black smooth stallion!
hey you reverberator of present definitions!
hey you pretty niggerito whom i have seen
since blackness penetrated the pores of my emotions!
hey you suntanned rainbow-skinned
ghetto preacher definitor
of new negritos:

    i love missing you in africa with me,
    to hear your hands clapping soulfully
    spanglispan spanglispan spanglispan
    phrases that make me think:
    i love missing you in africa!

    am reacting subtly to africa,
    i wish you were here with me, hermano,
    to make beauty with you, felipe,
    attending to the matters of Black Brazil
    creating definitions that redefine
    blackness again and again and all over again.
    god damn it, felipe!
    i love missing you in africa with me,
    nurturing my senses broader and broader, brother,
    making definitions out of eye scratch:
    "princely," "aristocratic," "gods"
    nothing but unifying statements.

    i love missing you in africa.
    africa misses the drums of your thoughts,
    she waits to give you citizenships:
    Oba of el Barrio
    Otun of Salsa
    she waits for you singing:
    what was made by slavery
    impossible,
    has been made by africa
    wonderfully possible!

to esteem thorns
of our major roots

were   luba   mi   ce
were   luba   mi   ce
were   luba   mi   ce
ohun   ti   aro   e   ko   ce   ce

the africa in pedro morejón

slowly descending, as if from the clouds above,
thinking of africa, i find myself enthralled!
rhythmic africanism swell and dwell inside
the fingers of my cuban mambo eyes.

the african rhythms i hear are native, native
from my cuban land, it is as if my guaguancó
was shipped to africa, when it was the other
way around, but nevertheless all my colors are the same.

i hear the merengue in french haiti
and in dominican blood,
and the guaracha in yoruba,
and the mambo sounds inside the plena
so close to what i really understand,
sometimes i think
that cuba is africa,
or that i am in cuba and africa at the
same time, sometimes i think africa
is all of us in music,
musically rooted way way back
before any other language.

yes, we preserved what was originally african,
or have we expanded it? i wonder if we have
committed the sin of blending? but i also hear
that AFRICANS love electric guitars clearly misunderstanding they are the root,
or is it me who is primitive?
damn it, it is complicated.

i had a dream that i was in africa,
it took me along time
to find the gods inside
so many moslems and christians,
but when i did, they were the origin of everything!
then i discovered bigger things,
the american dollar symbol,
that's african;
the british sense of royalty, that's african;

the colors in catholic celebrations,
that's african; and ...
ultimate ... listen here ... closer ...
come on ... closer ... sshhhhhh ...
two whites can never make a black ...
two whites can never make a black ...
two whites can never make a black ...
but two blacks, give them
time ... can make mulatto ...
can make brown ... can make blends ...
and ultimately ... can make white.

óyeme consorte, pero no repita esto,
porque si me coge el klu klux klan
me caen encima con un alemán
me esparrachan con una swastika
y me cortan la cabeza. pero, es verdad:
dos blancos no pueden hacer un prieto.

i went to africa and all of it seemed cuban,
i met a cuban and all of him was african,

this high-priest, pedro, telling me all of this
in front of an abandoned building.

savorings, from piñones to loíza

to combine the smell of tropical
plaintain roots   sofritoed
into tasty crispy platanustres
after savoring a soft mofongo
with pork rind pieces, before
you cooked them into an escabeche
peppered with garlic tostones
at three o'clock in a piñones sunday afternoon, after your body cremated itself dancing the night, madrugando
in san juan beaches, walking over
a rooster's cucu rucu and pregonero's
offering of wrapped-up alcapurrias
fried in summer sun . . .
hold yourself strong
ahead is the Ancón, the crossing to loíza . . .
you have entered the underneath
of plena, mi hermano,
steady rhythms that constantly don't change
steady rhythms that constantly don't change
tru cu tú   tru cu tú
tru cu tú   tru cu tú
tu   tu   tu

el moreno puertorriqueño
(a three-way warning poem)

qué voy a ser yo como moreno
puertorriqueño. preguntar
¿dónde está mi igualdad?
viendo novelas sobre morenos
esclavos, sin poder ver un
moreno en la pantalla. la
negra dorotea, el nené mingo,
papá cortijo, la morenita to-
masa, todos son blancos dis-
frazados, haciendo papeles sin
vida, haciéndose burla de mi
presencia. tratando de asimilar
mi color negroide para mejorar
la raza. ¿qué pienso yo?
¿qué pensarán mis compañeros?
les pregunto yo, ¿soy yo igual
o soy yo todavía esclavo?

ay baramba bamba
suma acaba
quimbombo de salsa
la rumba matamba
ñam ñam yo no soy
de la masucamba
papiri pata pata
loíza musaraña
bembón ay no canta
el cañonero es de acero
las puertas arrebatan
changó cambió color
es de la raza cumbamba
si no me quieres mi compay
te echaré flores
sin abundancia

ñam ñam yo no soy
de la masucamba
ñam ñam yo no soy
de la masucamba

summer wait

with the thought of
seven long months ahead
i await to see
your green ...
the many jam sessions
i took in, would they
give me enough winter
warmth? within leafless
trunk trees timidly towering
over my solitude, i await
your return, humming to the tunes
of dry leaves
slowly scratching cemented sentiments
making maraca-sound noises.

tumbao (for eddie conde)

tumbao is the spiritual rhythm of the nod
tumbao is the spiritual gathering of the congas
tumbao and tumbao met . . .

1.

tucutú pacutú   tucutú pacutú
tucutú pacutú   tucutú pacutú

aguacero de mayo que va a caer
aguacero de mayo que va a caer

ya estoy cansado de llorar
y estoy llorando
. . . llora como llore . . .
y estoy llorando
con la lengua afuera

2.

warm the fiery explotions
of hunger
come on cuchifrito juice
juana pena cries
boone's farm apple juice
juana pena dances
she shows slow curves
deep birth moans
a dead stomach that aches

3.

conguero
espíritu coroso
llamamba quimbembe
sin bajo
un hueco en el corazón
conguero . . . sonero
prisionero del parque arrabal
conguero
pito que pita

yuca que llama
salsa que emprende
llanto que llora
última llamada sin fuego
tumba que la tamba
tumba que la bamba baja
que pacheco se inspira
que ismael la canta
¡oh!   y el baquiné

4.

meaning childbirth
meaning sacrament of death
    instead of baptism
meaning solitude
meaning anger ...

5.

and the park   those ghetto parks
the living-room-kitchen
of many desperate souls
tumbao movements
street gutted salsa

6.

¡¡conguero!!
you bite frustrated
wine twistered definitions
and the winos find employment
for their wretched lives
reminiscing on the women
that left them because they
couldn't take it anymore

7.

conguero   despojero

tumbador   crazy boogie man

conguero   sonero

artista   manipulador
you can't take it aaahhh!
you can't take it aaahhh!
you can't take it aaahhh!
close your lips
expose your hands
give us your tired
your beaten your triste soledad
and sing for me ... allá en el africa central
            hay unos negros
               que se perdieron en puerto rico
trucutú pacutú   trucutú pacutú
trucutú pacutú   trucutú pacutú

8.

cowbells from empty wine bottles
empty congas   cemented hands
all these sounds
about words
around faces
coming from tito,
hermano mío,
coño, nodding on the streets

like un tumbao

summer congas (pregnancy and abortion)

from far away   i saw the congas playing
                 winos screamed
                 putas danced
                 soneros sang guaguancó tunes
the rest were spectators
ogling at themselves

from far away   i saw the congas playing
                 so hard that they were
                 buried in the pavement
                 the drummer creating sounds
                 from the sidewalk floor
                 the breeze carried them to far away ears

misunderstanding people
protested their fears
                 pigeons were fed
                 crap game found rhythm
                 lovers made music
                 system retaliated

from far away   i saw the congas playing
                 everyone walked to the tunes
                 tatatatá tutututú tucutupacutú
                 heroine sugar hands were exploiting
                 the last tune before winter oblivion

from far away   i saw the congas playing
                 junkies cooking
                 drummers now diluting . . .

congas catching cold,
uncultural weather . . .
trees received winter warmth . . .
spirits aborted a suffering
negrito, who became the winter drum
fire that reminisced those
three beautiful summer months.

from far away

and now
too cold

the salsa of bethesda fountain

the internal feelings we release
when we dance salsa
is the song of manu dibango
screaming africa
as if it were a night in el barrio
when the congas are out

the internal soul of salsa
is like don quijote de la mancha
classical because the roots are
from long ago, the symbol of cer-
vantes writing in pain of a lost
right arm, and in society today,
the cha-cha slow dance welfare

the internal spirit of salsa
is an out-bembé on sunday afternoons
while felipe flipped his sides
of the cuban based salsa
which is also part of africa
and a song of the caribbean

the internal dance of salsa
is of course plena
and permit me to say these words
in afro-spanish:
la bomba y la plena puro són
de Puerto Rico que ismael es el
rey y es el juez
meaning the same as marvin gaye
singing spiritual social songs
to black awareness

a blackness in spanish
a blackness in english
mixture-met on jam sessions in central park,
there were no differences in
the sounds emerging from inside
soul-salsa is universal
meaning a rhythm of mixtures

with world-wide bases

did you say you want it stronger?
well, okay, it is a root called africa
in all of us.

haiku

shanghai   streets   of san juan
split   between   two   realities
and   one   people

orchard beach y la virgen del carmen

and latin joe made the congas mad
    the sea waves receded
    there was a tornado in the sand
    the boardwalk cracked
    the people all stopped all danced
        conciously or subconciously

and latin joe and the congas were tripping
    the fingers named themselves
    meñique   anular   del
    corazón   índice   pulgar
    making heaven-hell sounds

    the sun sat next to the moon
    the birds stopped in mid-air

and victor quinteando was beautiful
    like cacique tunes keeping the rhythms

    the beer sold faster
    the grass was traveling at great speed
    the junkies found something
    that kept pace with their melodies
    the sounds raped all the virgins
    that were left

and ismaelito sang his father's tunes
    there was no difference
    Moti agua ...
    Yemayá Yemayá ... oh! oh! oh!
    Agua que va a caer
    Agua que va a caer
    Agua que va a caer

    the rain was coming down
    but the winds stopped it
and latin joe
and latin faces
    footmarks imprinted in the sand
    were even dancing

the congas were laid
and reached their climax!
tru cu tú pacutú
tru cu tú pacutú
tru cu tú pacutú
and nobody said it was inspired by
LA VIRGEN DEL CARMEN
coming out of the sun

canción para un parrandero

hombre sencillo   hombre sencillo
dime ¿qué regalo quieres
para la navidad?

hombre sencillo, lumpen . . .

"oye negrito, yo quiero CLARIDAD
bueno, negrito, yo creo en la Bomba para gozar

para la mujer	el hombre
para vacilar	la yerba buena, pero buena de verdad
para palés matos	el baquiné
para loíza	estar en su carnaval
para Puerto Rico	pues, para el puertorriqueño

tú ves, negrito, yo no pido más
tú ves, negrito, yo no pido más
vamos para la esquina a poner a los pobres
a gozar por un ratito nada más / a gozar por
un ratito nada más / a gozar por un ratito nada más /
a gozar para estar en paz / a gozar por un ratito
corto que tenemos y después . . . / tú sabes
lo que trajo el barco / no hay que decir más nada".

la música jíbara

derramando décimas con lágrimas
suplicándole a su mano "paciencia"
intrigando coordinación adentro del ojo
el cantor de las montañas sacaba el lo

pensando en el café perfumante
oliéndolo en montañas y arrabales
tirando la pava hacia la sombra
que congaba las tetas de cayey salía el le

y jorge brandon nos dice: "el jíbaro puertorriqueño
que siente amor por su tierra, quiere vivir en la sierra,
y ser de su casa dueño, vivir en la hamaca un sueño,
soñar con su patria chica, beber ron de caña rica,
jugarle todo a su gallo, robarse una hembra a caballo,
y morir como mojica". de jorge brandon salía el lai

lo   le   lo   lai   lo   le   lo   lai . . .

un minuto adentro de un segundo
sale la guitarra con su tiempo
infinito de perfección, con su
tiempo infinito de una canción.

¡oh! le vino en una inspiración, tal vez.
pero qué mucho camello paseando por
soles puertorriqueños ardientes.

doña cisa y su anafre

doña cisa estaba adentro la media madrugada
la noche entera se reflejaba en la luna
al són del verano, cogiendo el resfriado
que brinda el aire reumático, que camina en la pobreza.

la luna bailaba muy suave, buscando su reflección
en la tierra, buscando un alma o un instante
merecido a compararse con su belleza.

analfabeteando entre sílabas, la luna así decía:
   "cilusana   luanasa
   lusacina   lunacisa
   luna   cisa".
y también encontró el anafre, el instante
merecido y el alma entusiasmada.

parándose en un instante, transformada en dulce
voz de melodía, la luna así decía:

"ese ruido calentón, que escurre bacalaítos
hacía de Harina oro, doña cisa vende
bacalao para comprar pegao cuando el rico
la bota entregándoselo a los gatos".

'Bacalaítos',   entre su rugosa piel-dignidad.

'Bacalaítos',   gritaba ella, con ese entusiasmo
                    con ese querer.

'Bacalaítos',   sus ojos oprimían la leña
                    le daba fuerza al anafre
                    que vivió de lujo en el pasado
                    que vive de luto en el presente.

'Bacalaítos',   guardaba en su vejez una fierosa
                    juventud, dándole estímulo a calles
                    llenas de tristeza.

'Bacalaítos',   hechos con el sabor de manos
                    mezclando alrededor alrededor
                    y yo luna bailando a las tres

de la mañana. ¡oh, conocí
las nubes para disfrutar el buen
pensamiento a solas de mi soledad!"

doña cisa cantaba al són de la noche
perfumándola lentamente suavemente
dándole sabor al aire reumático
creando sin vanidad al nuevo jíbaro
que ponía firmes pies en el seno de
américa quemando ritmos africanos y
mitos indígenas.

"guarden sus chavitos prietos",
gritaba doña cisa,
"guarden sus chavitos prietos",
gritaban sus dedos borinqueños
mientras mordían las llamas del fuego
que quemaban esa noche loisaideña
escogiendo el camino

ni regular
ni suave
ni cósmico
pero el camino-carrito-cultural
del pensamiento típico.

doña cisa no refunfuñaba, no maldecía
el anafre gritaba de alegría cuando
el rasca rasca rasca que rasca
dientes jibaritos, chupándose las bocas
mordiéndose los dedos del sabor olor
bacalaítos fritos color oro
dignidad.

el sol salió besando a la luna
anafreándola con amor.

santa bárbara

entramos, todo está preparado
la música de changó era la luz del día.

entramos,   a la fiesta espiritual
             a lo rojo
             a lo santa bárbara.

baila   baila   dale vueltas
indios se levantan de su genocidio
negros se despiertan en sus espíritus
voces de las velas empiezan a hacer
dibujos espirituales en mis ojos.

hay algo, sí, sí, hay algo, algo
el vino está preparado, los cigarros se encienden
los santos se levantan a hacer fiesta
todo está preparado.

y martina
y el angel de la casa
se transforma en un indio burgués
y la señora de la casa está vestida de blanco,
rojo previene en nuestras vidas.

despojos   algunos suaves
            algunos fuertes
            algunos incrédulos

despojos en guayama
y la gente se levanta
esperando si santa bárbara
desciende de su trono
y cambia color a lo
negro coroso negroide.

dolores me vio sentirme incrédulo
yo no creía, no, no, yo no creía
pero había algo, y dolores se despojó
como una princesa taína, su cuerpo desnudo
con esa fuerza, dios mío, con esa fuerza,
esa fuerza, esa fuerza, esa fuerza que

> rompe la rapidez del viento
> y me hace sentir sudor
> y me hace escupir lágrimas
> alborotadas.

cogí un suspiro, paré de respirar
las venas se me querían salir,
dolores y martina se inspiraban,
me acosté al lado de una pared sobre
la puerta, cerré los ojos,
los abrí un poquito
las luces se veían pequeñas
empecé a moverme, moverme, moverme,
no sé por qué, ahí supe que me iban
a despojar, me concentré, levanté las manos ... y me fuí

> bailé como guarionex
> recité como juan borias
> canté como ismael

alguien real maravilloso
me tocó mi íntimo ser
creo que fue ELLA
extendiéndose las manos.

coreografía

I

Aída ... traje blanco ... escena verde ... luz amarilla

plenea
canta rumba en rumbón
suave las caderas
fuerte el coro del són
mantiene congas despiertas
se mueve con la brisa del sol

plenea
por las calles de loíza
del fanguito en el bronx

plenea rumbas de loíza
en el parque central

Aída baila majestad
se ve un barco de negros
ofreciendo ayuda a las
reglas de caridad ...
Aída baila entre pellejos
del conga cuero
collares a muchos colores ...
Aída su voz sonriente
le hace cariño al sol

por allí viene la noche,
¡Aída cantaba oh Aída cantaba!
se arropaba en blanco vestuario
las congas están calientes
las congas están calientes
se inspiró ... salió yemayá
congueros calentando
al són del són

¡Aída cantaba oh Aída cantaba!
sus mejillas acariciaban la noche
sus manos eran indios de asia

un clavito rojo en su bello cabello
... yemayá eh coro coro o yemayá
manos en cinturas
manos en pulseras
manos en collares
manos expresivas
todo el mundo en collares

Iván maraqueaba fuerte
Iván maraqueaba protectivo
maracas racas racas
impulsaban a Aída
inspiraban a Aída
exaltaban a Aída
su madre rezaba
al punto más alto
preservando bombas

acariciando plenas
soneando improvisaciones negroides
todo el mundo ... a cantar
                  a llorar
                  a despojar
                  a reír
                  a encontrar lo que es vivir

II

Aída ... traje colorado ... escena edificios ... luz amarilla

era viernes, Aída recorría
en el tren gusano
abastecido de miedo miedo
su cara asustada que
alguien la atracaría

Aída miraba la noche
en su corrida por calle simpson,
caras admiraban Aída:
ese rojo orgulloso de su andar
pero la luna estaba triste

escupiendo pedazos de nubes
triste vomitando el sol medio dormido
"¡qué horrorosa noche!"
"¡qué horrorosa noche!"
Aída decía

en la esquina, el vinillo ardiente
prostitutas-hermanas vivían la soledad
dentro de sus siete pellejos
Aída . . . . . . negra noche
Aída . . . . . . negra angustia

los celos de él
los celos vengativos
querían encarcelar su belleza
en control supremo
esas peleas que inspiraban Aída
a cantar la opresión de la bomba
en las caras dolorosas en nuestros hermanos:
los que cometen el delito de la aguja
por el tren de satisfacción

adentro de la sociedad
más baja más hundida
por esas calles de simpson
por esas calles de fox
y él se apareció de momento

sin hablar le entregó en las frases
de sus mejillas cortadas
por el frío calentoso
de una navaja que acariciaba
su bella cara y le sobaba la
sangre derramada en la cutis
infierno de la calle

Aída, ya flaca, despojada
en un lamento dolor
subía escaleras
llamando súplicas negroides
nadie la entendía y la sangre
roja de su tierna cara le corría

a su rojo traje—el ave de
siete muertos en ruedas murmullaban
al río ¡oh la negra sonera
sufriendo boleros pálidos y hondos
qué dolor, qué angustia!

sus manos en pulseras de sangre
se maraqueaban como un ala de
hoja muerta
sus mejillas aclimaban al negrindio
sus ojos miraban hasta el cielo
sin estrellas hasta el cielo de sucio
nadie presente
sola
qué extremo, ¿verdad?
qué extremo, ¿verdad?

y él no corrió
le gustó por un
diablo momento
verla sufrir   sin cantar
                  sin cantar
"eres mía   mía
me cantarás sólo a mí
              o
no le cantarás a nadie".

III

Aída ... traje marrón ... escena blanca ... luz amarilla

en la cama abortada
adentro del dolor
Aída gritaba gritaba sufriendo
muerte en esa cama
muerte en esa cama
muchos negros le rezaban
a su vida y no a su muerte
lloraban el dolor interno
se inspiraban en la venganza

su madre se pretendía fuerte
en preparación en preparación
recogiendo matas y hierbas
buscando a santeras y espiritistas
"Dios, no me la dejes sufrir
Dios, no la dejes sufrir
con la muerte. Dios, no me
desengañes, no me abandones.
Dios piadoso, por favor te
ruego, te ofrezco este hábito,
te doy mi alma entera. ¡Oh!
Dios potente me acuesto en tu
servidumbre, te doy esta promesa,
no me lleves la hija mía".

en la noche su espíritu se paró
sufriendo de dolor
recordando aquel momento
de Aída en inspiración
la vimos volando en su traje blanco
en su traje blanco de festejo
y voló del dolor y voló del dolor
yemayá las potencias de las súplicas
del mar le limpiaban con su virgen
caridad, las aguas buenas del morir
vivir le apoyó por su espíritu limpio,
le dio nuevamente su pelea

su espíritu le volvió a su cuerpo
en ese momento   momento tenso
con tantos ojos   que no eran ingratos
abrió los ojos   abrió los ojos
llamando a todos un fuerte abrazo
    "con Dios todos, sin Dios nada
    volveré a captar   volveré a cantar
    volveré a bailar   y perdón
    le doy a mi fiel amado
    que me comprenda
    que vi en su acto de violencia
    un acto de amor".

el sonero mayor

el hombre hablaba
se inspiraba desde
cárceles hoteles
extraños países

         "déjenme irme que es
         muy tarde ya"

un hit disco detrás del otro

         "para lo que tú le da"

cinco bolsitas de coca
porque estaba

         "en la triste soledad
         de mi celda yo compuse
         esta canción para ti"

parrandeaba las calles
de loíza, de la tapia
hablando de los espíritus y

         "negros carabalí que
         con su ritmo i na rará
         bailan así y dicen así"

y que quizás se habían perdido
en puerto rico, y siempre
por todo puerto rico
por el fanguito del south bronx
por las calles llenas de pobres
por todos los social clubs
se oía:

         SU VOZ ILUMINOSA
         EL SONERO MAYOR
         EL TEORÉTICO DE NUESTRAS VIDAS

él me dio, y le da
a muchos condenados en la tierra

su único momento
de placer y de alegría

"dime por qué me abandonaste
no me atormentes, amor, no me
mates, ten compasión dime
por qué"

y yo estaba pensando cuál era
la razón que él decía

"en este mundo si uno no se
alaba no hay quien lo alabe"

y ese hombre cuya voz enérgica
y poderosa le daban

"para lo que tú le das
tú le das tú le das
tú le das tú le das
palo, puño y bofetá"

nosotros bailábamos
sus cantos alumbraban,
en todos bembés
sus ídolos lo imitaban
había algo positivo
en su belleza
ismael y su swing maravilloso
me entiendes

"juan josé, pasé por tu
casa y te llamé. juan
josé como no me oístes
te pité"

pero creo que había un vacío
en su alma, a veces oíamos
sus canciones pero no lo que
él decía. solamente mi hermano
pablo y todos los compañeros
de la soledad y la ironía:

los de las cárceles ... los de fort worth ... los de lex.ky ...
los de la 110 ... los de la castro viña ... los del barrio
obrero ... los de martín peña ... los de puerta de tierra ...
los lumpen pobres de la tierra

veían a ismael como una luz
poderosa en nuestras vidas

en orchard beach
conocí a su hijo ismaelito
y cantaba   igual
y soneaba   igual
y se movía   igual
        igual que
        su padrecito

y pensé.

declamación

¡Oh! ... don Jorge ... JORGE BRANDON.
yo a ti, te veo ... en mis nubes,
quebrando el hilo de la imaginación
qué de prenda, diamante ... ilumina la vejez
en el día madrugante

¡Oh! ... don Jorge ... JORGE BRANDON.
pan que alimenta   sin pesares ...
canción del muerto vivo ... llanto de los que
lloran ... gritando ... sol de los pobres que luchan
ídolo de los héroes de patria
transformación a cualquier sufrimiento
pensador de todos ... orador de nadie

¡Oh! ... don Jorge ... JORGE BRANDON.
te quiero tal como nadie nunca te ha querido
eres como la canción de Rafael Hernández
como la palabra inspiradora de Pedro Albizu
el concepto del vocablo PATRIA que Luis Muñoz
le dio a los carreteros.

¡Oh! ... don Jorge ... JORGE BRANDON.
padre espiritual de todos ellos,
en tu poesía encomiendo mi madre,
mis hijos, mi patria, mi abuela ...
el pan nuestro de cada día dánosle hoy
y perdónanos nuestras deudas porque
tus décimas son lágrimas
tu vida es muerte en espíritu
tu espíritu es aliento al que te encuentra
tu fama es el futuro ... cuando ánimas
que conozcan grandeza, se cuelan a estudiar
la prosa de un santo

¡Oh! ... don Jorge ... JORGE BRANDON.
te toqué como Jesús fue tocado
por Verónica y sentí las palabras
poderosas del autor profeta
de las aguas santas.

¡Oh! ... don Jorge ... JORGE BRANDON.
¿en qué sitio apropriado
te escribo yo estas lágrimas?
donde el grito es de victoria
aquí en la arena del madison sq. garden
adentro, el luchador pedro morales
es un ídolo del pobre que lo acoge
y lo alienta en el desengaño romántico
de ganar entre los países más grandes
    entre las piedras olvidadas
    entre el mar profundo de bellezas
    entre el fervor del despojo de llamas

¡Oh! ... don Jorge ... JORGE BRANDON.
y ganó una ilusión, pedro morales
¡pero ganó un grito eterno!
¡un llanto admirable!
¡un suspiro de fuerza!
qué ... Dios mío, ¡Dios mío!
se quedaba ... nunca fue rechazado
ni vencido ...
¡los de abajo! ¡Oh, los de abajo!
desde allí escribe Brandon
y ese grito espiritual-poeta
nunca será reemplazado
en américa dirán,
"era el GRITO más alto".

¡Oh! ... don Jorge ... JORGE BRANDON.
a veces me pierdo entre brujos que hacen mal ...
me desanimo entre el bien que no progresa ...
me agito con almas que no creen en paz ...
pero te toqué, ... al tocarte mis hijos te tocarán, ...
las frases del ánimo en tu vejez, en tu experiencia
te piden el beso, ...
    el beso que no tiene otro igual
    el beso Padre de Borinquen
    el beso Madre-Corazón
    el beso de ... don Jorge ... JORGE BRANDON.